D0586629

The Tickle Ghost is somewhere near,
Can you see him? Can you hear?
He's slowly creeping up the stairs,
He'll try to catch me unawares.
But I can always hear his giggle,
Here he comes, TICKLE! TICKLE! TICKLE!

I laugh so much I nearly cry,
Now he's found somewhere to hide.
Is that him behind the curtain?
I think so but I'm not certain.
Yes it is, I hear a giggle,
Here he comes, TICKLE! TICKLE! TICKLE!

At last I manage to break free,
It's my turn now, he won't find me.
I'm in the cupboard on the landing,
Who's that on the outside, standing?
What's that noise? Is it a giggle?
Here he comes, TICKLE! TICKLE! TICKLE!

"Too much laughing," Mummy said,
"It's time your DAD put you in bed."
He kisses me and says goodnight,
He leaves and switches off the light.
But as he does I hear a giggle,
Here h   TICKLE! TICKLE! TICKLE!

913 000 00129617

For Nicky (Mummy), Flynn and Blake. B.M.

LONDON BOROUGH OF HACKNEY	
913 000 00129617	
ASKEWS & HOLT	28-Mar-2011
JF MCK	£10.99

First published in Great Britain in 2011 by Andersen Press Ltd.,
20 Vauxhall Bridge Road, London SW1V 2SA.
Published in Australia by Random House Australia Pty.,
Level 3, 100 Pacific Highway, North Sydney, NSW 2060.
Text copyright © Brett McKee, 2011.
Illustration copyright © David McKee, 2011.
The rights of Brett McKee and David McKee to be identified as
the author and illustrator of this work have been asserted by them
in accordance with the Copyright, Designs and Patents Act, 1988.
All rights reserved.
Colour separated in Switzerland by Photolitho AG, Zürich.
Printed and bound in Italy by Grafiche AZ.
David works on Arches paper in pen and Indian ink,
gouache, coloured and lead pencils.

10   9   8   7   6   5   4   3   2   1

British Library Cataloguing in Publication Data available.
ISBN 978 1 84939 246 4 (Hbk)

The TICKLE GHOST

David & Brett McKee

Andersen Press

"Where is he?" said Dylan.

"Where's he hiding?"

"Bedtime, Dylan," called Mum.

"Yes, Mum," Dylan called back.

"I'll see to him, dear," said Dad.

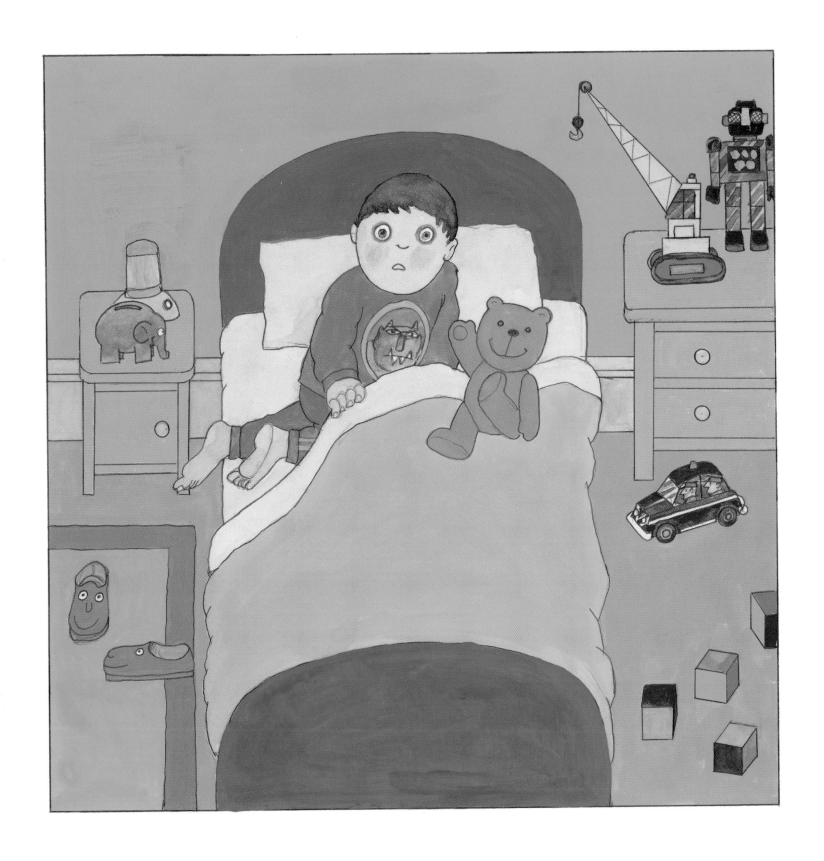

"Is he creeping up the stairs?"
whispered Dylan.

"Giggle! Giggle! Giggle!" the
ghost giggled.

"Tickle! Tickle! Tickle!" the
ghost tickled.

"Ha! Ha! Ha!" Dylan laughed.

"Daddy!" shouted Mum.

"Yes, dear," answered Dad.

"It's his bedtime," said Mum.

"Yes, dear," said Dad.

"There's too much noise," said Mum.

"It's not Dad, Mum," shouted Dylan.

"It's the Tickle Ghost," said
Dad and Dylan together.

"Tickle Ghost indeed," said Mum.

"Right, I'm coming up."

"Quick," said Dad. "She's coming up."

"Where are you?" said Mum.

"Are you hiding?"

"Giggle! Giggle! Giggle!" the ghosts giggled.

"Tickle! Tickle! Tickle!" they tickled.

"Ha! Ha! Ha!" they all laughed.

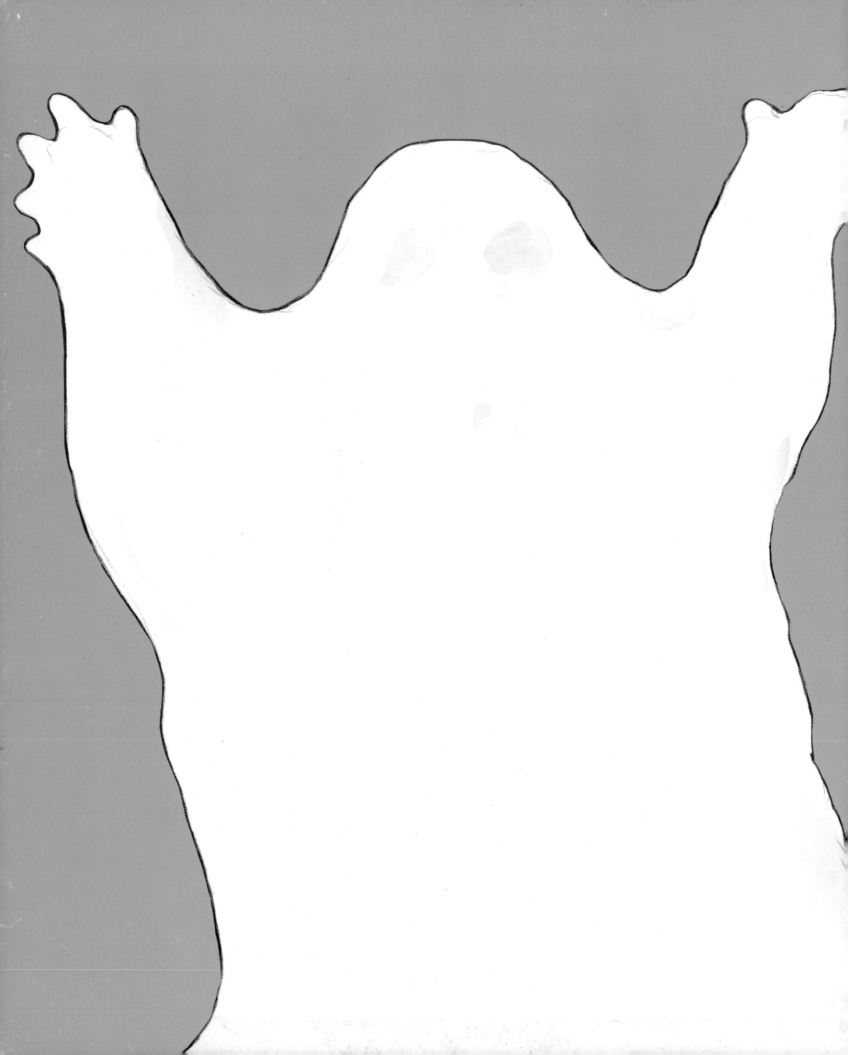